Conversations of Comfort
A Book of Poems

Sarita "Spirit" Durham

ENTEGRITY
CHOICE PUBLISHING

Dedication

I thank God who is truly a Father and a Daddy to me. You always welcome me with open arms during the hardest times in my life. You are always listening and willing to respond when I've called You. I am forever thankful to You.

Author's Note

My pain was the avenue that began my journey to healing through *Conversations of Comfort* with God. When you ponder where is God when life hurts; simply say, Hey God, I need to talk.

Contents

Wounded For Me

"But He was wounded for our transgressions; he was bruised for our iniquities: the chastisement of our peace was upon Him; and with his stripes we are healed." Isaiah 53:5

You were wounded for me
I'm sure the reasons I'll never see
But you were wounded for me
They never understood who you really were
But they brought you Frankincense and Myrrh
They beat you beyond recognition
But you lived above human traditions
You went into the synagogue to teach
But some hard heads you could not reach
You asked if they could pray for an hour
They didn't recognize your true power
They made up stories and then they lied
Yet for them— you hung, bled and died
As a result I have given my heart to thee
You didn't have to do it, but you were wounded for me.

I will Answer

"Call unto me, and I will answer thee, and shew thee great and mighty things, which thou knowest not." Jeremiah 33:3

Oh Lord, the enemy is after me
Mine eyes seek after thee
Lord, in your presence I humbly bask
You said you would answer if I simply ask
Lord, for you only do I seek
The plans you have Lord, let me peek
I'm humbling myself, unlike the peacock
At your door I stand and knock
Child, continue to seek my face
Come meet me in the secret place
For you, the enemy has a ploy
But in my presence there is much joy
Elevate your mind from off the ground
In the high place is where I'm found
Call unto me and I will answer
For "I AM" your life enhancer
Lord, I continuously call out to you
I couldn't hear you answer and now I'm blue
Child, my eye is not blind
You are always on my mind
Think back on times past
I answered you then and it won't be the last.

A Lost Rib

"For he who touches you, touches the apple of his eye."
Zechariah 2:8

I said in my Word that it is not good for the man to be alone
I made you from his very flesh and bone
You were the rib from his side
And there I wanted you to reside
Even though he has put you away
In my presence you can always stay
You are my very own daughter
I will not lead you into slaughter
A lost rib is how I feel
My heart, Lord, I need you to heal
My daughter, my daughter, I'm healing the hurt
Healing is yours until you are laid in the dirt
A lost rib is how you feel
To the enemy I've spoken, "No deal"
In my kingdom there is no such thing
So in my Presence let the praises ring
I knew you would be a great rib
Even before you were laid in a crib
"Lord, I'm a lost rib," loudly your cry rings
But in my kingdom, there are no such things.

Healer

*Indeed, I'll bring you healing, and I'll heal you of your wounds,'
declares the LORD, 'because they have called you an outcast and
have said, "It is Zion, no one cares for her!" Jeremiah 30:17
(ISV)*

Hey, why are you looking blue?
I've come to heal you
Pain, from your spirit came blurting
And I knew you were hurting
I AM here for you
I will heal and comfort you too
You don't have to be shame
Just call on my name
I need you to be in good health
And you are a person of wealth
I healed the woman with the issue of blood
I rescued Noah from the flood
I opened the eyes of the man who was blind
Healing you, I don't mind
You are the apple of my eye
In me does your healing lie
I sent my Son to heal all manner of diseases
I hear your supplications and decrees
If you decree healing from your mouth
I'll send healing winds from the North and South.

Rise Again

"Weeping may endure for a night but joy cometh in the morning." Psalm 30:5

They knocked you down
But could not destroy you
On your head sits a crown
They are going to keep coming for you
Touch not mine anointed I have said
They beat you down and left you for dead
You kept your eyes looking to the north
Then you heard me say, "Come forth."

Your sufferings are never in vain
You have endured enough pain
The World is waiting for you to win
The World needs to see you Rise Again!

You Were Created To Dominate

"So God created human beings, making them to be like himself. He created them male and female, 28 blessed them, and said, "Have many children, so that your descendants will live all over the earth and bring it under their control. I am putting you in charge of the fish, the birds, and all the wild animals." Genesis 1:27-28 (GNT)

You were created to dominate
But the woman is not your subordinate
My Power is in your hand
You are to subdue the land
I've tried to teach you who you are
Now I need you to raise the bar
Stop living below your means
Be a man and pull up your jeans
I remember us walking in the cool of the day
I'd like to do that again, if we may
You, my son, are a king in life
You shall reign without any strife
I love you more than the created birds
So please refrain from vain words
The power that you hold in your mouth
Can cause situations to go south
Speak life so dry bones can live
The breath of life to you I give
Go now son and don't be late
Responsibility and power are on your plate.

You Still Have Me

"I am praying to you because I know you will answer, O God.
Bend down and listen as I pray." Psalm 17:6 (NLT)

Hey, I've been calling out to thee
Did you not hear me?
From your spirit came blurting,
Words of despair because you are hurting
Yes, you've been through a lot
It was the enemy's plot
You still have me
I have not forsaken thee
My plans for you are very huge
Come, run to me, I'm your refuge
Don't duck, dodge and hide
Come with me and abide
Remember you still have me
My Spirit is calling out to thee.

I Forgive You

*"If we [freely] admit that we have sinned and confess our sins,
He is faithful and just [true to His own nature and promises],
and will forgive our sins and cleanse us continually from all
unrighteousness [our wrongdoing, everything not in conformity
with His will and purpose]." 1 John 1:9 (AMP)*

Lord I don't deserve this, because I'm not right
Especially after what I did last night.
You said that my sins were forgiven
But by my lust I have been driven
I've told you once and I'll tell you again
I do not remember your sins
I'm not concerned with that old mess
By my blood, you are my righteousness
You have to repent and turn away
Change your mind and do not sway.

Lord, I don't deserve to be blessed
Over your will and your Word, I have messed
Change your mind and elevate your thinking
Then my child, you won't feel stinking
Rise above this rut you are in
I have always called you my friend
You deserve all that I have to give
Dust yourself off now and live
Death and life are in your tongue
Speak life so you don't live like dung.

Blessed Beyond Measure

*"Thou wilt show me the path of life: in thy presence is fullness
of joy; at thy right hand there are pleasures for evermore."*
Psalm 16:11

It's not by might that you do these things
It's by the power that my Spirit brings
You've been strong and accomplished a lot
With my blood your soul I've bought
I paid a high price for your life you see
I know your purpose and destiny
Seek me out and you will find
The fulfillment, pleasure and peace of mind
*In my presence is fullness of joy
You won't find it in a material toy
You are blessed beyond measure
It has been my divine pleasure
You have the power to do anything
Just keep bringing glory to the King.

St. John's Wart

"In my distress I called upon the LORD, and cried unto my God: he heard my voice out of his temple, and my cry came before him, even into his ear." Psalm 18:6

Lord, I'm suffering with Depression
That's just your impression
I need St. John's Wart
No, you need to enter my court
I don't mean to be rude
Come to me and I'll change your mood
I lay down at night, and I can't sleep
Into my presence you need to peep
St. John's Wart will keep me calm
So will I, when you rest in my palm
St. John's Wart is the best
No, I AM! Rest on my chest
Lord, nothing is greater than thou art!
Well come to me, let me do my part
You really don't need St. John's Wart.

What About Me?

"The helpless call to him, and he answers; he saves them from all their troubles." Psalm 34:6 (GNT)

I see you struggling from day to day
My spirit calls out, Child why don't you pray?
I see you hurting and my heart hurts for you
I call you again, and you keep doing what you do
You call your friend, when you are about to bend
And still ultimately there is no end
You and your friend go out on the town,
But what you really need to do is bow down
I'm right here saying, what about me?
But you still chose to go party
The World has offered you everything
You still didn't find ME in the bling
Child, I'm calling your name so clear
I've told you that I'm always near
You finally realize that it's Me you need
And now you think you have to beg and plead
I heard you say, "Lord what about me?"
Child, I'm here holding on to thee.

Blue Holiday

"I will not leave you comfortless: I will come to you." John 14:18

Lost Loved ones
Lost jobs
Death is all around
I try to sit quietly and listen for your sound
The holiday is here
But I can't find any cheer
You said Pray, Pray, Pray
But still I find a Blue holiday
Dear soul, those things did not come by ME
Holiday or none, I'm mindful of thee
Yes Pray, Pray, and Pray is what my Spirit will say
For in doing so, you can eliminate the Blue holiday
Loved ones may be gone and jobs may be lost
Death may be around
But my love always will abound
With me, I've asked you to spend time
Come and see, My presence is sublime
Don't focus on a Blue holiday
Focus on ME and receive a royal payday.

Giving

"Give, and it shall be given unto you; good measure, pressed down, and shaken together, and running over, shall men give into your bosom. For with the same measure that you mete withal it shall be measured to you again." Luke 6:38

Giving is a gift
It gives you and others a lift
So through your life please sift
Take a moment and shift
Look in your heart and find compassion
Take that love and carefully ration
Love is a gift that comes from the Father
If you don't know Him, then with love, don't bother
Our ultimate gift is His son
So try giving, it's fun
It's not about the material things
It's about the love that giving brings
It doesn't take money to bless and give
Time is precious and not too expensive
Release some time and become addictive
Live to give and be re-la-tive
If the gift is true
It will bless me and you.

Your Name Is Special

"I knew you before I formed you in your mother's womb."
Jeremiah 1:5

Before you were created, you had a name
If you don't like it, your mother's not to blame
God knew you before you were planted in the womb
He'll still know you when you're placed in the tomb
Embrace the name that He has given
On your certificate it has been scriven
The name was whispered in your parent's ear
Prayerfully they received it with cheer
Maybe the transmission was skewed that year
Don't be angry, they simply could not hear
If you have a name such as Jezebel
Go to the Father and your "true" name He will tell.

No Compromise

*"But they that wait on the Lord shall renew [their] strength;
they shall mount up with wings as eagles; they shall run,
and not be weary, [and] they shall walk, and not faint."*
Isaiah 40:31 (AMP)

Girl, your body is God's temple
So let's keep this simple
His Spirit dwells inside
And in Him you should abide
Please do no compromise
Keep some things as a surprise
Don't allow him to give you a carriage
Make him wait for marriage
He should treat you like a Queen
Between your legs he should not glean
Hold off on that for a while
Don't let him give you that unplanned child
Waiting is not complex
Don't be eager to give oral sex
Don't increase the population
By giving in to copulation
Wait, wait, and wait some more
If he's begging, please ignore
Your body is the temple of the Holy Ghost
So for disease and other spirits, don't play host
Carry yourself with honor and delight
Another statistic is the devil's plight

Don't let him give you a temporary thrill
Wait on God's plan that He will fulfill.

Wait On Your Mister

"Delight thyself also in the LORD; and he shall give thee the desires of thine heart." Psalm 37:4

My sister, my sister
I know you feel lonely waiting on your Mister
God knows who you need and knows your fears
When he comes you will dry your tears
If you wait on the LORD, things will be better
Take some time out and write God a letter
Explain to HIM that you have a need
I promise you, He'll answer in deed
Set your eyes just a little bit higher
I promise you, He'll grant your desire
I'll pray for you my dear sister,
As you wait patiently for your own Mister.

Is This For Me?

"For the gifts and the calling of God are irrevocable [for He does not withdraw what He has given, nor does He change His mind about those to whom He gives His grace or to whom He sends His call.]" Romans 11:29 (AMP)

Lord, is this for me?
How can it be?
I have not been all that I can be
Child, look to me
I am blessing thee
The plans that I have for you are due
There are no religious works for you to do
I've tried to be faithful and true
Most days I'm so busy that I miss you
I pray that you can understand
I realize that you are not a man
Correct, I AM not a man and I don't lie
The plans that I have for you will not die
If I said it, then so shall it be
In all things, always look to me
Yes child, this is for you
My Son's Blood has purchased this too
Again Lord, are you sure?
I'm no place near pure
The gifts that you have for me are good
Bless my friends too, if you would
My righteousness and my blood have made it so

This is really not a show
I asked you to stand and endure
I never said you needed to be pure
For you this gift has been in place
Never forget the power of my saving grace.

Manifestation Time

"You will arise and have compassion on Zion, for it is time to be gracious and show favor to her; Yes, the appointed time [the moment designated] has come." Psalm 102:13 (AMP)

Over are the days of gestation
Now is the day of manifestation
You've waited and fought a good fight
Over is your midnight
You've asked, and asked and asked again
Yet your answer was in the making
Life has not been easy
But it was worth it
My answers aren't cheesy
And you will birth it
It's manifestation time and you will see
The manifestation came only through me.

No Money, No Food,
No Place To Stay

"Because the poor are plundered, because the needy groan, I will now arise," says the LORD; "I will place him in the safety for which he longs." Psalm 12:5 (ESV)

No money, no food, no place to stay
Focus your attention on me today
LORD, you said that you would provide
Since you didn't believe me, let's take a ride
I have a seat for you in Heavenly places
You keep walking at many different paces
Remove your pride and look deep inside
I AM the one who makes all things new
Raise your faith because I'll do it for you
No money, no food, no place to stay
Are merely distractions to make you stray
Slow your stride, let me provide
In me is where you should abide.

Am I The Only

"It is in vain that you rise up early and go late to rest, eating the
bread of anxious toil;
for he gives to his beloved sleep." Psalm 127:2

Lord, I feel as if I'm the only
You said I'm not alone, but I am lonely
I sit up late with a lack of sleep
I'm hurting so bad, I can't count sheep
With me I eat, sleep and watch a movie
LORD, this season is not groovy
LORD, I'm grieving my loved one, you see
This person is no longer here with me
LORD, I lost my job today
Oh my God, I have bills to pay
My body, I need you to touch
LORD, it's painful and hurts so much
In this situation, am I the only?
I'm sitting at the bottom and boy it's lonely
Try not to dwell on being lonely
I promise you that you're not the only
Most of my children won't come to me
I'm always here to comfort thee
There is nothing about you that I don't know
My compassion is what I'm trying to show
It is in vain that you go to bed late and get no rest
All these situations are simply tests
In my Word, I promise to give you sleep

There is no need for you to try to count sheep
You lost your job and have bills to pay
Have faith in Me, I always say
My Spirit is there by your side
In my presence you need to abide
Come here to me if you would only
Let me fill you up so you won't feel lonely.

A High Price To Pay

"He gave himself for our sins in order to rescue us from this present evil age according to the will of our God and Father."
Galatians 1:4 (ISV)

I visited this home that was filled with laughter from above
They seemed to be knitted in love
I stood by and watched as they made lots of pun
They were having so much fun
I wondered if they even knew you
Your Spirit was grieved and mine was too
As my spirit began to take a dive
You told me that I should not strive
I tried to introduce you but they didn't have time
I was hoping that my little light would shine
I said that you were my Savior and Lord
The look on their faces said they were bored
In You they seemed to have no desire
As they snuggled up cozy by the fire
I explained to them that in me was fire that burned deep inside
I said, in my Father's Kingdom is where they should abide
I heard you whisper for me to say,
"If it wasn't for the Savior they wouldn't be celebrating this day"
You told me you loved them anyway
Because your Son had a high price to pay.

Single Father

"Sing and rejoice, O daughter of Zion: For, lo, I come, and I will dwell in the midst of thee, saith the Lord." Zechariah 2:10

Raising a daughter is such a charm
She will learn what to look for and not be alarmed
Teach her to always pray,
So when that person comes along and wants to play
My voice she will hear and she'll know the way
Never fear knowing what to do
I'm your Father and I love you
Give her to me and she will be fine
After all, both of you are mine.

Single Mother

"A Father of the fatherless and a judge and protector of the
widows is God in His Holy habitation." Psalm 68:5 (AMP)

Lord, being a single mother is not fair
My child looks around for his father and he's not there
Sometimes when I take my child to visit his father
I ponder in my mind, why bother?
I understand that things happen in this life
I'm trying to walk with you and have no strife
Morality wasn't on my mind in the making,
Reality has kicked in and a toll it's taking
Mother, you should realize that I am the child's Father
I'm the only life giver and there is no other
I knew the child before he was formed in the womb
Lead the child to me and watch him bloom.
Teach him to love no matter the cause
He will seek me for his applause
Teach him to seek me for every need
His expectations, I will supersede
Single mother, the fruit of the womb was my reward
For any sin you've committed, you have been restored.

The Waiting

"Wait and hope for and expect the Lord: be brave and of good courage and let your heart be stout and enduring. Yes, wait for and hope for and expect the Lord." Psalm 27:14 (AMP)

Lord, sometimes it seems that you are taking so long to
deliver
I wrestle with doubt while trying not to have a sliver
I trust you but it's getting very hard
I guess the heavens I need to bombard
The question that I ask is "Lord, when?"
My conversation is more consistent than now and then
Basking in our presence is a real task
I find myself walking and continuing to ask
Well you said, ask, seek and knock
But it appears for my blessing, there is a block
It's in the waiting that you find strength
I'm God alone, with time I don't see any length
Hey, in me you need to just trust
In my Kingdom, trust in a must
If you focus on me and keep your faith strong
Your waiting will diminish and won't seem so long.

Left Over Mud

"So God created man in his own image, in the image of God created he him; male and female created he them." Genesis 1:27

Let us make man in our own image
The words that I spoke to myself
I'm not Santa Claus so I have no need for an elf
Though you were formed from the Earth
I was present at your birth
At times you may feel left alone
But all your sins I will atone
You were created with the best material
At birth, there was no tutorial
I use everything that I created and it was ALL good
Even if you were raised in the hood
You are mine, made from the dirt
At times I speak and I am very curt
Take heed that you have much value
Walk with a very tall statue
Keep your head up knowing that I care
If you go astray, I'll meet you there
You were not made from leftover mud
Move out your own way, so I can watch you bud.

Happiness vs Joy

*"And the randsomed of the LORD shall return, and come to
Zion with songs and everlasting joy upon their heads: they shall
obtain joy and gladness, and sorrow and sighing shall flee away."*
Isaiah 35:10

Don't settle for happiness when you can have joy
I know you are hurting and boy oh boy
The plans I have for you are very weighty
My plans don't change even if you're eighty
Happiness is temporary but joy is stable
Please call on me because I'm able
You asked if you could have some fun
But when things got hard you tried to run
Clear your mind and prepare for gladness
I've told your enemy to stop the madness
The joy that I have is unspeakable
Humble yourself and remain teachable
Don't chase the decoy
Wait for the real McCoy
Forget about happiness and get some joy.

My Plans

"For I know the thoughts that I think toward you, saith the Lord,
thoughts of peace, and not of evil, to give you an expected end."
Jeremiah 29:11

I planned your life before you were born
Live through it and do not mourn
I planned out the life you now live
To you, my pleasure and purpose I give
From the beginning I declared the end
You dear one, I call friend
Before I perform in the Earth
I tell the prophet and you give birth
I AM God and there is none like me
I gave my only son for thee
Great are the creations on my hands
You are the one to carry my plans
My plans are not by any man's might
So with man I choose not to fight
You are special and worth a great prize
So get up and let your spirit rise
I love you and on me you should pull
Do this so our joy might be full
To live a good life are my plans for you
So listen and obey and let me do what I do
I never said that life would be painless
But let me lead you and don't walk around aimless
I know that you will not live perfect

I still consider you mine elect
Remember that you are never alone
While living my plans, I'm your backbone!

Love Is Contagious

"He that loveth not knoweth not God; for God is love."
1 John 4:8

The Love of God is contagious
To live without God is outrageous
His love is untainted and pure
That's a love that is sure
Love is what revived the world
After the fall it was in turmoil

I sent my only begotten son
When He died, "it" was done
I call out to you in the night
Sometimes you may feel it's not right
Often, I wake you up from sleep
I wanted to converse, but not be deep
Smile at the person passing by
It's something they cannot buy
Love is what the world needs
For love their soul bleeds
Reach out to me because I am love
I AM who you are seeking, and I come from above.

Turn Back To Me

"Let your conversation be without covetousness; and be content with such things as ye have: for he hath said, I will never leave thee, nor forsake thee." Hebrews 13:5

Hey God, I'm wondering why we're so poor
I don't know, I've opened the door
I've turned my back on thee
I don't feel your love unconditionally
Well draw yourself close because I AM here
You said the same thing yester year
Trial after trial, and I'm in the same condition
Child, you need to change your position
You see, I'm God and I'm God alone
I'm the only one sitting on my throne
Your thoughts of me are much skewed
Talk to me; my answers are not cued
You've turned your back due to unbelief
I sent my son to offer relief
Open up and let me in
Time is short and my grace is running thin
Get rid of the anger and the dirty attitude
Replace it with a heart of gratitude
Everything in life is about a choice
Make a decision and follow my voice
I'm not a man that I should lie
But moments like these, my hands you tie
Turn back to me, you were doing so well

Until you listened to the enemy and the lies he'd tell
Turn back to me, I AM right here
I turned my back on thee
Can you forgive me?
I'm waiting on you and Heaven will rejoice
Turning back to me is your choice.

My Toothless Wonder

"Lo, children are a heritage of the LORD, and the fruit of the womb is his reward." Psalm 127:3

Powerful are the creations of my hands
The glory I have is not man's
As I sit here and ponder
I gaze at this toothless wonder
Am I able to create a baby?
I sit back and think, maybe
The making of a baby is no mistake
This toothless wonder I will not forsake
This child is mine, whom I will protect
He will grow to receive honor and respect
Teach him all the things he should know
Put him on the path that he should go
If he should stray, he will come back
I'll protect him from every attack
He will grow up and do great things
He'll enjoy the pleasures that life brings
Live your life and be bold
Do great things 'til you are old
Even if you decide to go yonder
You'll still be my toothless wonder.

Turned Around To Say "Thank You"

"And one of them, when he saw that he was healed, turned back, and with a loud voice glorified God." Luke 17:15-16

LORD, for me you do so much
Some look around as if there is no such
I say thank you Jesus
You didn't come to appease us
The Heavens' voice will bombard
I'm saying all along, thank you Lord
Hallelujah is the highest praise!
And with that, my praise is raised
For so many you came and were willing to die
A sacrifice that's higher than the sky
LORD, thank you, thank you and thank you
To you, only is my praise due
I was quickly on my way,
And I turned around to say,
Thank you.

Child Of The Most High God

"Then Nebuchadnezzar came near to the mouth of the burning fiery furnace: he spoke and said, 'Shadrach, Meshach, and Abednego, you servants of the Most High God [El-Elyon] come forth, and come here: Then Shadrach, Meshach, and Abednego came forth out of the midst of the fire." Daniel 3:26 (WEB)

I am a child of the Most High
Yes you are, and I AM nigh
Adversity comes but I am strong
LORD, the wait seems so long
Don't focus on Earthly time
I said you are a child of mine
You are a child of the Most High
All your tears, I will dry
You were not made from my flesh and bone
I'm the Most HIGH, El-Elyon
I will protect your heart
I'll extinguish every fiery dart
The enemy will not run roughshod
Because you are a child of the Most High God.

P.O. Box 453
Powder Springs, Georgia 30127
770.727.6517

info@entegritypublishing.com
www.entegritypublishing.com